Miriam Monnier

Just Right!

Translated by
J. Alison James

A Michael Neugebauer Book
North-South Books
New York / London

This is me.
Sometimes I am big.
But sometimes I'm still little.
Actually I'm not exactly sure.

Mother says, "You are my big girl. You can climb
the stairs all by yourself."
But I still like her to carry me like a baby.

But then she says, "You can't have gum.
You are much too little to chew it."
But I can chew gum. I can make the
loveliest long gum strings. I just
can't blow bubbles yet.

When I eat with my fingers, Mother says, "You eat like
a baby. Use your fork like a big girl."
But it doesn't taste as good that way.

One day we went shopping and the shopkeeper said,
"You are such a big girl, helping your mother. Here,
have a lollipop." I liked that!
But Mother didn't.
She said, "Lollipops are
bad for your teeth."

After that I walked a little bit behind her so I could lick my lollipop in peace. But a lady came up and said, "You are too little to be out on your own. Where is your mother?"
All this was making me angry. Was I big or was I little? Everybody said something different.

At home, the boy downstairs was standing in his
doorway. When I asked him if he wanted to play,
he said "I can't play with you. You are too little!"
And he shut the door in my face.

I went home feeling sad and asked my mother if we could play robbers. But she said that she had lots of things to do and that I was a big girl and could play by myself.

That was it. I'd had enough. I stomped to my room,
slammed the door and threw myself on the bed.
I didn't want to hear another word.

Mother came in and asked me what was wrong. I began to cry. "I don't know if I'm too big or too little!" I told her.

She took me in her arms and said
"You aren't too big or too little, either.
You are just the right size! And I love
you more than anything in the
whole world, no matter if you are
big or little, naughty or nice,
grumpy or sweet!"

The boy downstairs was waiting outside his door the next time we came home, but I didn't want to play with him. My mother and I held hands and went up the stairs together.